Hey Parents,
We're Going to the Beach is a Sing-Along-Story set to the rhythm of "The Farmer in the Dell." If you and your child like this book, make sure to check out "We're Going to the Farm," by Nancy Streza and illustrated by Adam Pryce.

Text Copyright © Nancy Streza 2015
Illustration Copyright © Adam Pryce 2015

All Rights Reserved. No portion of this book may be reproduced without express permission from the publisher.
2015 First Edition

© 2017 Bilingual Edition by Xist Publishing
All rights reserved
This has been translated by Lenny Sandoval

Published in the United States by Xist Publishing
www.xistpublishing.com
PO Box 61593 Irvine, CA 92602
ISBN-13: 9781532403613 eISBN: 9781532403620

Nos Vamos a La Playa
We're Going to the
Beach

Escrita por
Words by Nancy Streza

Illustrations by Adam Pryce
Ilustraciones de

x*ist Publishing

Nos vamos a la playa
Nos vamos a la playa
Hi-ho La playa
Nos vamos a la playa

We're going to the beach
We're going to the beach
Hi-ho-the beach-e-o
We're going to the beach

We're going to pick up shells
We're going to pick up shells
Hi-ho the shell-e-o
We're going to pick up shells

Recogeremos conchas
Recogeremos conchas
Hi-ho las conchas
Recogeremos conchas

Arrastraremos algas marinas
Arrastraremos algas marinas
Hi-ho las algas
Arrastraremos algas marinas

We're going to drag the seaweed
We're going to drag the seaweed
Hi-ho the weed-e-o
We're going to drag the seaweed

Construiremos un castillo
Construiremos un castillo
Hi-ho castillo
Construiremos un castillo

We're going to build a castle
We're going to build a castle
Hi-ho the castle-o
We're going to build a castle

We're going to dig the moat
We're going to dig the moat
Hi-ho the sand-e-o
We're going to dig the moat

Excavaremos una fosa
Excavaremos una fosa
Hi-ho la fosa
Excavaremos una fosa

We're going to chase the gulls
We're going to chase the gulls
Hi-ho the chase-e-o
We're going to chase the gulls

Perseguiremos las gaviotas
Perseguiremos las gaviotas
Hi-ho gaviotas
Perseguiremos las gaviotas

Buscaremos a los cangrejos
Buscaremos a los cangrejos
Hi-ho cangrejos
Buscaremos a los cangrejos

We're going to look for crabs
We're going to look for crabs
Hi-ho the pinch-e-o
We're going to look for crabs

Escalaremos en las rocas
Escalaremos en las rocas
Hi-ho las rocas
Escalaremos en las rocas

We're going to climb the rocks
We're going to climb the rocks
Hi-ho the rock-e-o
We're going to climb the rocks

Montaremos en las olas
Montaremos en las olas
Hi-ho las olas
Montaremos en las olas

We're going to ride the waves
We're going to ride the waves
Hi-ho the wave-e-o
We're going to ride the waves

Atraparemos un pescado
Atraparemos un pescado
Hi-ho pescado
Atraparemos un pescado

We're going to catch a fish
We're going to catch a fish
Hi-ho the fish-e-o
We're going to catch a fish

Competiremos con la ola
Competiremos con la ola
Hi-ho la ola
Competiremos con la ola

We're going to race the wave
We're going to race the wave
Hi-ho the jump-e-o
We're going to race the wave

We're going to watch the sunset
We're going to watch the sunset
Hi-ho good night-e-o
We're going to watch the sunset

Observaremos el ocaso
Observaremos el ocaso
Hi-ho el ocaso
Observaremos el ocaso

Made in the USA
Monee, IL
24 April 2023

32323379R00019